DRACULA
BEYOND STOKER

Issue 3.5

DBS Press

Dracula Beyond Stoker
Issue 3.5

Tucker Christine
editor

Edward G. Pettit
consulting editor

Published by DBS Press
ISBN - 978-1-963391-00-8 (Paperback)
ISBN - 978-1-963391-01-5 (e-book)
February, 2024

www.dbspress.com
www.draculabeyondstoker.com

Letter From the Editor to the Reader

31 January

My Dear Loyal Reader,

In an alternate universe, the book you're holding would have been Issue 2.5. The initial plan was for half-issues to serve as bridges between main books, containing stories that didn't quite fit with the others for various reasons. However, when "Another Dracula?" fell into my lap, I couldn't let it go and 2.5 seemed like the best place for it.

Going forward, these shorter volumes will fluctuate between new stories, like those in this volume, and fascinating, found reprints. I have several fun, almost forgotten works that I'm hunting down for you which I hope to be able share in the near future.

In the meantime, please enjoy these exciting new Renfield and Bloofer Lady stories. In C.L. Werner's "There Are Such Things," a preternatural inquiry society founded by Lord Holmwood investigates the circumstances surrounding their own origins with horrifying consequences. And then we get a glimpse of a quirky, misunderstood Renfield who just can't give up the asylum life in Ross Baxter's "Renfield Hall."

We'll be back in a few short months with all new tales of Dracula's Brides!

Tucker

There Are Such Things
By C.L. Werner

S o you're telling me there's such a thing as a vampire?" Lloyd Cavendish didn't bother to temper the amused contempt in his tone when he posed the question to Major Edward Ravencroft.

"I'm certain the major means a peculiar personality who is able to leech the vitality of those around him. A 'psychic vampire' if you will," interposed Sir Darren Martinson-Lee, desperately trying to defuse the animosity he sensed in the atmosphere. The more gray hairs that peppered his head, the more Sir Darren appreciated tranquility at these monthly meetings of the London Society for Preternatural Inquiry.

Ravencroft, a tall and imposing man, leaned against the mantle of the fireplace and swirled the brandy at the bottom of the glass in his hand. "I do not muddle my words, gentlemen," he pronounced with imperious authority. "What I say is precisely what I mean." He took a slow, measured sip of his drink, indifferent to the provocation of his audience.

The London Society for Preternatural Inquiry boasted a small and exclusive membership, conducting their meetings in the upper rooms of a house on Brook Street in the prestigious Mayfair district each fortnight. At present there were ten men assembled in the drawing room indulging in after-dinner drinks and listening to Major Ravencroft's opinions on various occult subjects. While the members had been quite willing to indulge topics such as the chemical foundation of ectoplasm or speculation that apparitions functioned at a higher harmonic resonance than physical matter, they met claims of vampirism with a more skeptical outlook.

"This is no longer the nineteenth century, Major," Dr. Allan Pettigrew objected. "We're twelve years into the twentieth. It's well past time to discard such obsolete notions as vampires and werewolves." The plump physician stroked his waxed mustache as he leaned back in his high-backed chair. "Next you'll be telling us that leprechauns are stirring up the unrest in Ireland." Dr. Pettigrew frowned when his flippant remark brought sparse chuckles from the others.

Ravencroft fixed his stern gaze on the physician. "If you'd spent any time in Ireland, you'd know it needs no supernatural agency to provoke grievances, only the indifference of Whitehall." He walked across the room and discarded his empty glass on the side table. "But we weren't discussing little people or lycanthropes," he stated, returning his attention to the men scattered about in the chairs and divans arrayed around the room. "We were on the subject of vampires …"

"Which you insist are physical, material entities," Cavendish quipped.

The major made the briefest nod of his head at his detractor. "They are. An evil presence … force … influence, whatever word you choose, takes possession of a recently deceased body and by its malign power infuses it with a simulacrum of life. This corpse … revenant, is then capable of animation. It moves, sees, hears, walks just as a living person would."

"Then I would say that your 'revenant' is a living person," Pettigrew grumbled. "Many people in the past have been incorrectly declared dead only to revive later. To a superstitious mind, believing the person already dead, they would credit all sort of malignant influences to these occurrences. Nor is it to be wondered when the recovered person may well have become mentally deranged by such a horrible ordeal, no longer acting the way they had before 'dying', perhaps even gripped by total amnesia of who they are." The doctor smiled at the men around him. "Of course, with medical advances, such aberrant incidents are now exceedingly rare."

"In England, or France, certainly," Maurice de Grande, a short, pale-haired man seated across from Pettigrew said, a French accent just edging his speech. "Even in America they seldom inter the living by mistake with the dead. But you are forgetting that many places are not so fortunate as to have refined and orderly systems in place as yet." The little Frenchman took a quick jolt of his brandy. He stared down into his glass as he continued. "Then you are forgetting those who would deliberately incite such atrocious mistakes. In Haiti there are witch doctors, the *bokor*, who will curse a person to die, then quickly exhume them so the victim can be reanimated as a *zombie*."

There were a few guffaws as the members considered the unfamiliar word. De Grande looked up and shook his head. "No, no, I assure you that it happens. Of course the zombie has not truly returned from the grave because the bokor's victim has never truly died. The power of his curse isn't a thing of witchcraft, but of chemistry. It is a mistake of the supposedly enlightened mind to sneer down our noses at supposedly primitive beliefs. How often has science 'discovered' a remedy that was already known to the indigenous peoples of an area? So it is with the zombie powder used by the bokor. It is a terrible poison that puts the victim into a death-like coma. Then, after the burial, the bokor digs up his victim and applies a second poison, one that partially revitalizes the body but leaves the mind in a dull, numbed condition. He then hires out his near-mindless zombie to landowners to act as simple brute labor." The Frenchman paused, his expression grim. "You can scoff, but I have seen it. In Haiti there are laws that stipulate if someone poisons another person and that person is then buried, the crime shall be judged to be murder ... regardless of whatever happens after. I ask you, if the victim is truly dead, then what can possibly happen after to change that?"

"That may all be true, Maurice," Cavendish said, "but the major was arguing for the existence of vampires, not zombies, and it is his contention that these are corpses when they go into their tombs, not victims of catalepsy."

Ravencroft raised an eyebrow and favored Cavendish with a thin smile. "Despite your attitude, you've gleaned the essence of my statement."

Sir Darren sighed in exasperation, his efforts to preserve a tranquil atmosphere collapsing all around him. "But surely you don't maintain that a dead body can be brought back to life after the ethereal vitality has been extinguished? All of us here are open-minded. The London Society for Preternatural Inquiry was established to investigate psychic phenomena and ghostly manifestations, but you're asking us to entertain an entirely different matter."

Wagging one finger like a school room lecturer, Ravencroft reproved the older man. "That is not the position that the Society's founder took." The major pointed at a large portrait on the far wall. It depicted a middle-aged man dressed in the style of a decade past. His handsome features were distorted by a grimness, the stamp of loss and tragedy from which the subject of the painting had never recovered. "Lord Godalming most assuredly believed in the existence of vampires."

"It was the horror of that sort of thinking that haunted Arthur Holmwood to an early grave," Dr. Pettigrew commented.

"We owe much to Lord Godalming," Sir Darren was quick to remind the others. "He donated the vast occult library he'd collected to the Society and left a generous endowment for our continued research. Whatever his personal beliefs may have been, we can certainly agree that he was a seeker after the truth."

"Any eccentricities Lord Godalming might have had, I blame entirely on that German," Cavendish said.

"If you mean Professor Van Helsing, you'll find he is a Hollander, not German," de Grande corrected. "Nearly a hundred years old, but still active in his research. I believe he has been living in Rome. Consulting the Vatican's archives, as I understand."

Dr. Pettigrew laughed. "Research? Bah! The man was a crank twenty years ago and I don't doubt that he's still a crank. It was an ill wind that blew that charlatan into Holmwood's life when he was at his most vulnerable! I wonder how much money the Dutchman was able to extract out of him over the years."

Ravencroft's eyes took on a cold intensity. "Not enough to compensate Van Helsing for the service he has done the world," he said. The major turned a challenging look upon the skeptics. "I had expected a more genuine feeling of curiosity from this society. Instead I find the same attitude of trepidation and doubt as I did when the Hermetic Order of the Golden Dawn expelled Crowley from its membership."

"Another rascally fraud," Cavendish declared.

"Perhaps," Ravencroft conceded, "but a man of ideas — ideas that the Golden Dawn rejected without even the slightest investigation."

"How do you investigate the utterly fantastic?" Pettigrew countered. He gestured at the major. "How, for instance, do you go about securing proof that vampires exist? Not conjecture, not philosophical argument, but material, tangible proof of what you're claiming."

Ravencroft nodded up at the portrait of Lord Godalming. "If you want proof, we could do no better than to revisit the very tragedy that is responsible for the establishment of this Society." He paused, studying the room for the impact his words might have on his audience. "We return to the matter that so disrupted Arthur Holmwood's life. In 1887, the woman to whom he was engaged died suddenly. Van Helsing, in his books, has made veiled references to terrifying events in that year. Pursuing those hints, I was fortunate enough to gain access to certain diaries of some of the principals involved in those events. The death of Miss Lucy Westenra wasn't natural. What followed after her death was most certainly unnatural."

"Anecdotal evidence is not evidence," de Grande said, his voice not unsympathetic to Ravencroft. The Frenchman tilted his head towards Pettigrew and Cavendish. "It will need more than the recollections of even the most respected authority to convince someone who must see and experience for themselves."

"Yes," Cavendish agreed. "If you want me to accept such a thing as a vampire, you must show me one." The words were meant as a joke and a murmur of laughter spread among the Society.

Ravencroft did not find the challenge amusing. "That could be arranged … if you have the courage to do what is necessary." Again, his imperious gaze swept across the room. "If there are brave men here, then I can show you where a vampire can be found right here in London." He gave a respectful bow to Lord Godalming. "Our founder's tragedy will be our guide."

Sir Darren's visage paled. The old man stood up from his chair. "Surely you're not proposing to violate his fiancée's tomb."

"Only by such a violation can I provide these men with the proof they need," Ravencroft said. "Sentiment is a restraint upon the inquiring mind. How many generations was medicine held back by moral scruples that refused permission to study dead bodies? As a result many died who might otherwise have lived."

"But if all you're saying is true, then what should we find in Lucy Westenra's tomb?" de Grande asked. "By Van Helsing's papers, he says the vampire was executed. That means we would only find a desecrated corpse, not a living vampire."

Ravencroft paced before the fireplace, the flames throwing his shadow across the wall. The interplay of light and dark made Lord Godalming's portrait glower at the room. "The undead exist in a state that is beyond natural laws as we understand them. They can be destroyed, but they cannot be killed." He pointed his hand at the ceiling as he emphasized his point. "In destruction, what remains of them lies dormant, like a seed, only awaiting the right conditions by which to rise again. The details of what Van Helsing and his companions did to subdue the vampire that was Lucy Westenra are grisly enough, but it seems Lord Godalming wouldn't permit the action by which the undead seed itself could be annihilated. The corpse should have been reduced to ashes and scattered over moving water. This was not done, and so, if we've the courage, we may venture into Highgate Cemetery this very night and see for ourselves the evidence."

"That would still only mean viewing a desecrated corpse," Dr. Pettigrew said.

Ravencroft smiled at the physician. "That is where we must rely upon your contribution, doctor. You are affiliated with Charing Cross Hospital. We should need a pint, perhaps two, of blood to conduct our experiment."

Pettigrew blanched at the request. "What ... what sort of .... experiment?"

"I mentioned a certain notorious occultist," Ravencroft explained. "Among his unpublished material Aleister Crowley has written is a monograph on the subject of vampirism. Both how to destroy the undead and *the means by which they might be resurrected*." The major's defiant eyes roved once more across the room. "If this Society would see the proof they demand, all that is required is the courage to follow me into Highgate ... and two pints of human blood."

By necessity the Society had to conduct what Major Ravencroft morbidly described as their 'field experiment' in the dead of night. The custodians of Highgate were hardly likely to approve of the activities the men had planned and so the campaign would have to be conducted in a clandestine manner. To decrease their chances of being discovered as they slipped past the wall that enclosed the graveyard, it was decided that the group would consist of only five members of the Society. With Ravencroft were his chief detractors, Dr. Pettigrew and Cavendish. To balance them out was the slightly more sympathetic Frenchman de Grande. Old Sir Darren, whose connections to Scotland Yard would prove advantageous should they be caught trespassing, rounded out the company.

"Rather thrilling, isn't it?" Sir Darren quipped as the men stole down the narrow pathways between the stone crypts and marble monuments. There was a sparkle in his eyes and the blush of excitement in his face. Cavendish darted him a sour look and gave an imperative wave of his hand, motioning Sir Darren to keep the electric torch he carried pointed at the ground.

"This is really too much," Pettigrew grumbled. "It was all well and good to discuss this in a theoretical manner back in Mayfair …"

"Yet here you are, carrying an oh so macabre package," de Grande chuckled, nodding at the physician's black handbag. "Risking the notoriety of incurring the attentions of the gendarmerie." He tutted in mock disapproval.

"Perhaps they might think Dr. Knox is on the prowl again," Cavendish said, unable to resist a jab at Dr. Pettigrew. For all their mutual disdain of Ravencroft's theories, there was no love lost between the two skeptics.

Ravencroft gave his companions a reproving look. "Frightened children laughing in the dark to show how brave they are," he said. "Here, among these darkened mausoleums, perhaps my theories regarding vampires aren't so absurd to you."

Sir Darren shook his head. "That's an unfair remark," he sputtered. "The members of the Society have all made excursions to places just as disquieting as Highgate. More, I'd argue. Why, I myself have stayed overnight at Borley Rectory four times. Cavendish and de Grande spent twenty-four hours at the infamous 50 Berkley Square house."

"What about yourself?" Dr. Pettigrew challenged the major. "You're a rather recent member of the Society. What experiences have you had with the paranormal, or is everything merely theory with you?"

Somewhere among the thick underbrush that sprouted between the tombs, a furtive rustling began. Cavendish swung about, sending the beam of his torch full upon the cause of the noise. A large fox, its eyes glowing in the light, stared back at the men for a moment before dashing away into the shadows, the bright tip of its brush visible long after the rest of the animal vanished into the night.

"There are Chinese and Japanese who'd say we were being spied upon by a malevolent spirit," Ravencroft said, nodding at the animal as it fled. "To them, the fox has the same sort of ill-reputation that the wolf does in our own traditions." His face took on a somber look. "An interesting coincidence, given that vampires are supposed to be able to transform into bats and wolves and other creatures of sinister reputation."

Ravencroft gestured for the men to follow him down the narrow pathway. There was a fork in the path ahead, the statue of a cloaked angel with folded wings looming at the end of the juncture. Its marble hand seemed to point to beckon to the trespassers. A trick of shadow caused the angel's eyes to move as the men approached. Sir Darren shivered in his heavy coat and muttered a sigh of relief when they turned to the left and the statue faded from sight.

"We were discussing my qualifications," Ravencroft said. "My family can boast relationship to Alexander Ravencroft, a witch hunter active in the days of Cromwell's Commonwealth. Of course, even earlier than Alexander there was Agatha of Sussex, who was reputed to be a witch herself. You might say the Ravencrofts had a foot in both camps." The sparkle dimmed in the major's eyes. "My own experiences have been more direct and less erudite than your own. While I was posted in India, I saw many weird and curious things. A yogi who could ignite a bundle of sticks simply by gripping them in his bare hand. A fakir in Calcutta who could be locked inside a box and then appear outside the cage five minutes later. Oh, no trickery there, I assure you, for he could perform this feat without any preparation and even from inside a safe that was loaned for the purpose by the regimental command.

"There were other, more diabolical incidents," Ravencroft continued. "Somewhere my name became associated with supernatural incidents, and I was sent to look into all manner of phenomena, officially to debunk the events and pacify the public. Certainly some haunted houses proved to be merely bad plumbing, over-active rodents in the rafters, or unsound foundations. But there were others that couldn't be so easily dismissed. Some of them were deadly. In particular there was a gruesome tower in Mahabad where the locals continued to perform what is termed a 'sky burial.' Corpses were carried into the tower, left exposed on the roof so that they might be devoured by vultures. There was a murderous presence that lurked in the vicinity of that tower, reputed to be the spirit of a phansigar who was hanged during the campaign to eradicate the Cult of Thuggee. The killings were quite real, I assure you."

"What was the cause of the killings?" de Grande wanted to know.

Ravencroft turned and regarded the Frenchman for a moment. "We were never sure, but close examination inside the tower disclosed a hidden alcove in which a man's body was found. Quite dead, but equally obvious that the corpse was remarkably preserved. I had the head removed from the body and the killings stopped."

"A vampire?" Sir Darren asked.

The major shrugged. "It would be too much to state that categorically. But the killings *did* stop."

Ravencroft halted and indicated a crypt on their right, its front boasting a Greek facade with Doric columns and a sharply slanted roof. A brass plaque set above the door bore the name 'Westenra' and beneath it, the epithet 'Lady Godalming'. "We're here, gentlemen."

Solemnly, Cavendish and de Grande removed the pry bars and hammers from the packages they carried. With a last lingering look at the cemetery to assure themselves there was no watchman around, the two set about working to open the sealed door.

"Lend a hand," Cavendish huffed at the others. "This door is stronger than it looks."

"It was made not simply to keep people out, but to keep something in," Ravencroft remarked as he joined them in trying to force an opening.

"Everything is more proof of your outlandish theory," Dr. Pettigrew complained as he helped de Grande force the pry bar deeper into the gap they'd managed to create. "It's clear Lord Godalming loved this woman. It's natural he would want her remains protected."

"Hardly what you'd expect from a man who'd killed a monster," Sir Darren said, tilting the beam of his torch to shine upon the nameplate above the door.

"Lord Godalming loved the mortal woman, not the vampire she became after death," Ravencroft stated. "I believe that Lucy Westenra was the 'bloofer lady' who stalked Hampstead Heath and preyed upon children. A vampiress of ..."

The major's words trailed off as the heavy stone door suddenly gave way, toppling backward into the crypt's gloom with a tremendous crash that echoed like thunder within the tight confines of the tomb. Sir Darren shone the light across the interior. Cobwebs heavy with dust drooped from every corner, dangling in long strings like moldering draperies. Elaborate scrolling was visible on the walls, carved vines that curled together in intricate patterns. From the ceiling, an iron fixture was suspended upon a heavy chain, the nubs of old candles lingering in its proliferation of sconces.

It was the ponderous object at the center of the vault, however, that commanded all but the most fleeting attention. An enormous stone sarcophagus, its sides adorned with the same Greek stylings of the exterior crypt. A massive stone lid, its surface dominated by a sculpted cross, sealed the sepulcher. Carved above the cross was the legacy "Lucy Westenra, 1868–1887, Rest in Eternal Peace."

"This is it. I mean, really it," Sir Darren shuddered. He turned an imploring look toward Ravencroft. "You don't ... I mean we aren't ..."

"After coming all this way, I'm for seeing it through," Dr. Pettigrew grumbled. He hefted the case he was carrying. "I raised a few eyebrows asking for this. At least allow me the satisfaction of embarrassing the major when this mad scheme doesn't come off."

De Grande raised a hand in warning. "Perhaps it *would* be prudent to stop now. It was all fine to laugh and ridicule before, but now we are ..." He shrugged, stumbling to find the English for the sentiment he wanted to express. "At the very least we should be guilty of desecration, a betrayal of the Society's founder." He pointed at Ravencroft. "But if you're right, then we would be reviving a monster ..."

Ravencroft nodded. "Indeed, we would." He set down the case he'd been carrying. Opening it, he exposed a curious array of implements, including a sharpened wooden stake and a stout mallet. "Don't think that I didn't come prepared. What we revive we'll quickly put down again. Afterwards we'll take those measures Lord Godalming refused to take. Then the vampire will be destroyed for good." The major smiled at de Grande. "If it makes you feel any better, you may hold this." His hand dipped into the case and withdrew a large silver crucifix and gave it to the Frenchman. "Faith in the Forces of Good has ever been the counteragent to the Powers of Darkness. A vampire is repulsed by the image of the cross when it is held by someone who believes in its power."

"And the rest of us?" Cavendish asked. "What do we do to protect ourselves?" The question was put in a jesting manner, but there was a tinge of unease in the skeptic's eyes.

"I doubt a man of your sensibilities would be inclined to trust in a cross," Ravencroft stated. "Still, there are other protections. Not as effective, but of some value just the same." He handed Cavendish a garland of garlic bulbs, then produced another for Pettigrew. "According to Van Helsing, the aroma of garlic is repugnant to a vampire and will, at the very least, cause the undead to keep their distance."

"Does Van Helsing have any other helpful advice?" Pettigrew stared dubiously at the garland before slipping it over his neck.

"Only by what he suggests in his account of the Westenra tragedy," Ravencroft replied. He gave his companions a stern look, demanding their complete attention. "The fiend that killed Lucy Westenra wasn't, in Van Helsing's opinion, an ordinary vampire but something he designated as a 'king vampire.' A creature possessed of all the terrible hunger and might of the undead, yet which retained the intelligence and personality it possessed in life. A devilish abomination he named as Count Dracula." The grisly name sent eerie echoes through the crypt, as though a thousand ghostly voices were calling it back to the men as a warning.

"Van Helsing thought that just as the sire was mightier than the typical vampires of Hungary and Germany, so too would any undead created by Dracula belong to a more powerful strain." Ravencroft shook his head. "Van Helsing attributed hideous abilities to this Dracula. Transformation into wolves, bats, even into intangible mist. His strength … beyond that of any ten men …"

"Twaddle," Pettigrew declared. "The Dutchman is mad, and so are you for lending any credulity to this rigmarole. Let's get this over with before we all catch pneumonia!"

Ravencroft shrugged. "As you wish, Doctor." He gestured to Cavendish and de Grande. "Use your pry bars to push aside the lid. Sir Darren, keep the light on the sepulcher. Doctor … be ready to pour the contents of your bag upon the … contents inside the casket."

With grim resolve, the men set about the tasks assigned them. De Grande and Cavendish set to with their pry bars, the grating sound as metal scraped against stone reverberating off the walls and ceiling as they struggled to free the ponderous lid. Bit by bit, the cover was raised until finally it reached a critical point. Cavendish dashed aside as the huge stone upended and came sliding towards him. The lid slammed into the floor, splitting into several large chunks as it broke apart. The roar of its destruction was still echoing when the men crept forward to peer into the sepulcher.

"Good God," Sir Darren gasped as the light fell upon the interior. "They really did think she was a vampire!"

The body of Lucy Westenra had decayed so that there was little left except bones and a gauzy litter that had once been a shroud. The skeleton was preserved enough that the broken ribs were readily evident, a black crust around them to show where a long-rotted wooden stake had been hammered down into the heart. Even more stark was the unnatural positioning of the head as it stared down at the rest of the bones, the skull having been detached from the neck and simply set back down at the head of the casket.

Ravencroft leaned forward and brushed away the detritus from the hole in the chest. He worked his fingers into the wound, wrenching out a blackened stump of wood. He tossed this aside. "I don't think the ritual will work if we leave a stake through the vampire's heart."

"You … you mean to go through with this?" The torch in Sir Darren's hand shivered, throwing the light up into Ravencroft's face.

"It's the only way to make believers of you," the major declared.

"*If* you can pull off this magic of yours," Pettigrew scoffed. The physician leaned over the casket and began rapping on its bottom, ears keen for any sound that would indicate hollowness. Any place where Ravencroft might have some sort of magician's trick hidden.

"A disgraced aristocrat named Courtley discovered this ritual in an unexpurgated copy of *Cultes des Goules*, the arcane tome composed by the Comte d'Erlette and quickly suppressed by the Church," Ravencroft explained. "Courtley was quite convinced of the book's accuracy and the efficacy of the rites it contained. The ritual we'll be performing describes the restoration of the dead by means of a few essential salts. I think, with the complete corpse at our disposal and the benefit of a vampire's unholy vitality, we have more than sufficient materials for the ritual."

De Grande scratched his chin, his visage betraying his mounting trepidation. "Yes, perhaps we can do this thing … but should we?"

"Bother this nonsense," Pettigrew snapped at the Frenchman. Returning his attention to Ravencroft, he held up the bottles of blood he'd brought. "What do I do with these? Pour them over the skeleton?"

Ravencroft gave a solemn nod. "Yes. Be certain to get a little on every bone. Leave no part of the body unattended." As the doctor began to work, Ravencroft drew a paper from the breast of his coat and began to recite the strange, slobbering cadences of an alien language, a tongue even the most learned of his companions couldn't identify.

At first it seemed that nothing was happening. Sir Darren began to relax and a scornful satisfaction worked its way onto the faces of Pettigrew and Cavendish. Then the men noticed a change within the casket. Slowly, so gradual that they at first thought it only a trick of the light, a red mist began to form around the old bones.

The investigators looked on in silence as the mist expanded to become a ghoulish fog, billowing and undulating within the confines of the sepulcher. Abruptly, from beneath the scarlet veil, a hand thrust itself upward. It was a delicate, feminine hand, with tapered nails and a milky paleness to the skin. For all its seeming delicacy, as that hand grasped the edge of the sepulcher, so strong was its touch that the stone cracked and sent shivers of dust dripping to the floor.

"Stop, Major! Stop this!" de Grande cried out.

The sound of the Frenchman's voice enervated the thing within the casket. The red fog was abruptly disturbed by the surge of a body lurching upright. The men had a brief glimpse of a slender, shapely woman, the bloom of her voluptuous youth tainted by the ghastly pallor of her flesh. The silky black tresses that cascaded down across her shoulders and the vivid crimson of her lips were the only contrast to the ghostly tone of her skin.

For just a moment, the shape rising from the grave was that of a beautiful woman. Then the enticing vision was shattered. The vampiress opened her eyes, black pits devoid of warmth and humanity. The terrible orbs snapped to the figure of Ravencroft. Her lips curled back to expose long, sharp fangs. The major dropped the page he was reading from and leaned down to retrieve the hammer and stake.

Before Ravencroft could grab the weapons, the vampiress uttered a wolfish growl and sprang at the officer, plunging across the crypt with the ease of a panther. Ravencroft crumpled beneath her. He screamed once before the sharp fangs were digging into his throat. He managed to grab the hammer and swung at the creature's head. It cracked against her skull but failed to even dislodge the monster's teeth. He didn't have opportunity to swing again, as the vampiress seized his arm with one hand and snapped it like a twig.

"Good God!" Sir Darren shrieked. He threw the electric torch to the floor and fled from the crypt, Cavendish hot on his heels. Pettigrew, showing unexpected valor, drew a revolver from his pocket and moved to help Ravencroft. His shots plowed into the vampiress, searing into the pale flesh of her back. The undead tore her teeth from the major's limp form and glared at the doctor.

Seeing the inefficacy of his bullets, Pettigrew turned to run, but didn't make it as far as the door. Lunging back to the sepulcher, the vampiress picked up one of the fragments from the lid and hurled it at the fleeing man, casting the fifty-pound mass as though it were no more than a child's ball. The stone slammed into Pettigrew's back. He flopped to the floor, his spine broken, his limbs scratching at the air with the impotence of a crushed insect.

The vampiress turned from the dying physician, her eyes fixing upon the last mortal within the vault. She recoiled at sight of the cross de Grande held in his trembling hands. Then a cold, merciless smile spread across her ghastly face. She noted the tears that streamed from the Frenchman's eyes, the rapidity of his breath, the stench of his fear as it dripped down his legs. In two steps she closed upon de Grande and swatted the cross from his grasp, sending it spinning into a dark corner of the crypt. Terror had driven any semblance of faith from the man's mind. Slowly, savoring the moment, the vampiress pressed her lips to his neck, teasing his skin with her tongue, setting his blood racing still faster. Then, gradually, she dug her fangs into his throat and began to drink.

Lucy Westenra was famished after her long sleep. The three men lying within her crypt didn't satisfy her thirst. After drinking her fill, she remembered the two who'd fled at the instant of her revival. Perhaps she could still find them if they'd become lost in the mortuary maze of Highgate. She stepped out of the crypt and spread her arms wide. Only a moment did the pale beauty of the woman stand exposed in the moonlight. The next instant there was only the form of a huge gray bat taking wing.

The vampiress flitted above the shadows of the cemetery, her inhuman gaze piercing the dark to detect even the smallest ember of life. She'd find the fools if they were still here.

And if they weren't, there was always Hampstead Heath and the bounty of the bloofer lady's old hunting grounds to reap.

Exiled to the blazing wastes of Arizona for communing with ghastly Lovecraftian abominations, **C L Werner** strives to infect others with the grotesque images that infest his mind. He is the author of over forty novels and novellas in settings ranging from Warhammer, Age of Sigmar, and Warhammer 40,000 to the Iron Kingdoms, Kings of War, Beyond the Gates of Antares, and Zombicide: Black Plague. He has also written 'The Get of Garm', an official story featuring Robert E. Howard's Solomon Kane which appeared as a serialized prose story in Marvel's *Conan: Serpent War*. Most recently he added the Marvel Universe to his chronicle of misdeeds with the prose novels *The Sword of Surtur* and *Three Swords* from Aconyte Books. His short fiction has appeared in several anthologies, among them *Rage of the Behemoth*, *Shadows Over Avalon Volume II*, *Kaiju Rising*, *A Grimoire of Eldritch Investigations Volume I*, *Edge of Sundown* , *Shakespeare vs Cthulhu*, *City of the Gods*, *Write Like Hell: Kaiju*, *Marching Time*, and several issues of *Tales from the Magician's Skull*.

Renfield Hall
By Ross Baxter

I'm going to need to stop for the toilet soon," muttered Liz, glancing up from her mobile phone.

"Just another ten minutes," sighed John, starting to lose patience with Google Maps, the North Yorkshire road network, and with Liz in particular. "There's a layby ahead, maybe you can go behind one of the dry stone walls?"

"Do you think I'm an animal?" Liz shot back accusingly.

John said nothing, glancing back at the small map displayed on his phone. The reviews on Airbnb had warned of difficulty in finding the place, which, together with poor mobile signal, contributed to the overall low score their destination received. Given the state of his finances, poor reviews actually helped, making Renfield Hall a cheap place to stay for their summer weekend break. All he needed to do was find the damn place.

"Hey, I think I can see it," said John, suddenly excited. "Up there on the hill."

Liz looked up, scanning the wooden knoll and the large dark building partly hidden by ancient trees. "Finally," she murmured.

John gladly placed his phone back into his jacket pocket; looking at the map whilst driving presented problems on the narrow winding lanes, and twice the car had almost come to grief with itinerant sheep wondering on the road.

"It looks a bit grim," said Liz.

John shrugged. "I thought that was what you wanted? You said you wanted to stay somewhere interesting, and finding an old asylum converted into a guest house seemed to fit the bill well."

"Yeah, I suppose you're right," she conceded. "It's just a pity that it's in Yorkshire and not on the Costa Blanca in Spain."

"Maybe later in the year, when I've found a better-paying job," offered John. "But let's make the most of it, it does look an interesting place, there's plenty of nice walks and pubs, and Whitby isn't far."

"True," agreed Liz.

John slowed the elderly car as they approached a long drive leading up the hill to the left. "Renfield Hall, no trespassing," he announced, reading the weather-beaten sign.

Liz said nothing as they slowly drove up the rutted track towards the gloomy four-storey building ahead. Early Victorian, the hall had the austere lines of something built for function rather than aesthetics. Small barred windows marked the four floors, all set back in the gritty local sandstone blocks which had weathered over the years to a mix of dark matte grey. Dry stone walls separated the gardens from the surrounding sheep pasture, although the same unkempt grass grew on both sides. John pulled the car to the left, tires scrunching on rough gravel as he parked by a single small Honda at the end of the drive.

"I'll get the bags," smiled John, hoping that Liz would brighten up a bit now that they had arrived.

She waited for him as he retrieved the two small suitcases from the back seat, and followed him to the thick panelled front door. Opening the heavy door, she let him through.

Inside lay a barren hallway, and a desk behind which sat a callow youth, smoking and absorbed in her phone. She glanced up in surprise, quickly stubbing her cigarette out and taking the earphones from her ears.

"Mr. and Mrs. Ryder?" she asked, hiding away the half-empty packet of cigarettes in a drawer.

"We're not married," Liz answered sharply.

The pale teenager looked at her with a blank expression.

"I'm John Ryder," put in John. "This is my partner Liz. We're booked in for two nights."

"Yes," replied the girl, looking down at a large open ledger on the desk in front of her. "You have two rooms, bed and breakfast, leaving Sunday."

"Two rooms?" queried John.

"Yeah. All the rooms are small, and can only fit a single bed in. We only have ten rooms, all on the first floor. They are the old cells, which have been refurbished. All are partially ensuite, with their own toilet and washbasin, and there is a separate bathroom at the end of the corridor with a shower and bath."

"Okay," mumbled John, surprised at not picking up that information when he originally booked.

The teenager opened a drawer and took out two large keyrings. Both had a large ancient iron mortice key, and a smaller, shiny, modern key. "The old key is for your room door, the shiny key for the front door here. Rooms eighteen and nineteen,"

"I thought you said there are only ten rooms?" asked Liz.

"Only ten rooms in public use. The place has lots more, but most are on the second and third floors, which you don't have access to. Breakfast is between eight and nine in the breakfast room, last door on the left," she said, pointing down the hall.

"Are there many others staying here," said John.

"No," replied the girl without interest. "Just Mr. Renfield."

"Is that who the hall is named after?" asked Liz.

"I guess," shrugged the girl. "He took it over when the asylum closed."

"When was that," Liz pressed.

The teenage gave another shrug of her thin shoulders, even less interested this time. "Not sure. Ages ago."

Liz frowned, having more questions but seeing the girl had no interest in hearing them.

"Okay then," said the girl, standing and retrieving her cigarettes from the drawer and putting them in her jacket pocket. "The stairs over there lead to your rooms. I'll see you at breakfast tomorrow."

"Are you leaving?" asked John.

The girl nodded. "There are no more guests expected, so I can go. Have a nice stay. Oh, and smoking is not allowed in the building."

John stared at her in confusion. "What if we need something?"

"Just use the buzzer in your room, it's a red button by the door."

John and Liz watched in surprise as the youth nonchalantly put on her black denim jacket and walked out of the front door, slamming it behind her.

"You did want to stay somewhere interesting," chuckled John.

"Looks like we got it," Liz smiled. "Let's see what our separate cells are like!"

Liz led the way to the stairs. Like the reception and hallway, they were bland and functional, as if decorated from left-over supplies from a third-rate public library or minor town hall; all magnolia and beige. The first floor proved similar, a row of ten doors on the left hand side, with a large open area on the right with an assortment of mismatched chairs, sofas and tables. Large curtain-less windows looked out over the grassy farmland, letting in light which reflected from the shiny chocolate brown linoleum which covered the floor. At the far side a couple of closed doors sat, one marked bathroom, the other with a no-entry sign on it.

"Wow," whispered Liz. "I think we've just time-warped back to the nineteen fifties!"

"More like eighteen fifties," remarked John, glancing around the austere space.

"Shush, someone might hear us!"

John looked around. "There are only ten rooms, and all the doors are open. I think she said we're the only guests."

"But she mentioned Mr. Renfield, upstairs."

"I'm sure he can't hear us. Let's check out our rooms."

She followed him down the row of open doors to where he paused.

"Wow," said John, tapping his knuckles on the dark green door. "They're steel, and even have a barred flap at the front."

Liz peered at the flap. "It opens from the outside!"

John laughed. "So the guards or nurses could look in I suppose. A voyeur's dream!"

"Oh my god, look inside," cried Liz, pointing at the tiny single bed, small wooden standalone wardrobe, ancient radiator, and stainless steel toilet and washbasin. "It's like a prison cell!"

"To be fair, it did say that on the advert, which was one of the reasons we booked."

"I know, but I didn't expect it to be this Spartan."

John laughed. "As long as the bed is comfortable, I like it."

Liz went in and closely inspected the stiff white bed linen and hard pillow, turning them over and peering closely. "Well, the sheets are clean, and feel starched."

John grabbed her and bungled her onto the bed. "How about we loosen them up?"

Liz pushed him off, laughing. "I think you need to ply me with drinks first — the mattress feels like concrete."

"It does a bit, and there is no way we can both sleep together without falling out, it is so narrow," grinned John. "So, let's find the nearest pub and get plastered!"

"I want to see if the other room is any better," said Liz springing up.

John followed her next door, which was an exact copy of the first room. He looked out of the small barred window out towards the bleak moors. "Great view though."

"How am I expected to sit on that?" Liz cried, pointing at the low shiny steel toilet bolted to the painted brick wall. "There's no seat!"

"Your hot ass will soon warm it up!" John joked.

Liz shook her head. "And there's no toilet paper."

"Then maybe we press the buzzer, and see what that does," said John, moving towards the red button recessed in the wall by the metal door.

Liz shrugged, so he pressed it. No sound came, and no indication that it had been pressed, but immediately they heard a door open outside the room. Both peered out to see an open door at the end of the floor, and a small man shuffling slowly towards them. He looked to be ancient; bent forwards and thin as a rake, but well dressed in an ill-fitting tweed jacket and tie. With white hair carefully combed and slicked back from his pale and wrinkled forehead, he seemed to be ready to be going out to a formal party.

"You rang?"

"Err, yes," said John, somewhat disconcerted. "Sorry. There's no toilet paper in one of our rooms."

"I know," said the old man, holding up a white toilet roll. "I wasn't sure what type you'd want, so I've bought one of each."

John glanced at Liz, even more disconcerted. "I didn't know there was more than one type?"

"Oh, yes," the old man assured him. "Hard or soft. Most of our guests seem to prefer the hard type, but you two don't look like my normal clientele, so you may want the soft one."

"I'm not sure I understand," said Liz, seeing the look of confusion on John's face. "Who are your normal clientele?"

The old man smiled, fixing her with dark eyes which, although rheumy, seemed quick and alert. "Many seem to enjoy the idea that this place was once an asylum, and that the rooms have changed little since that time. They seem to revel in it, acting out sick fantasies, pretending it is still an institution for the insane. It is that type of guest who demand the hard toilet paper."

"Oh," said Liz, wrinkling her nose in distaste. "Soft is fine for us."

"I'm pleased. I find the idea of fantasizing about being in an asylum quite disagreeable. I can assure you that staying in an establishment like this for real was never the stuff of fantasies. However, I need the income, so people like that are still welcome to stay."

"So, you must be Mr. Renfield, the owner?" John asked, extending his arm towards the old man.

Renfield looked at the proferred hand for a moment, then shook it hesitantly. "I am."

John let go quickly, surprised at how cold Renfield's hand felt. "I'm John, this is Liz."

Renfield smiled warmly at Liz, shaking her hand with much more enthusiasm.

"Welcome to my home."

"It's an interesting building," said Liz, quickly disengaging from Renfield's tight grip.

"It's been my home for most of my life," the old man nodded. "When the local health authority finally closed it, I had just enough money to buy the place and continue to live here."

"That's good," said John. "Did you work here for the health authority?"

"No."

An uncomfortable pause followed, which John quickly tried to fill. "How close is the nearest pub?"

"The Strugglers Arms is only ten minutes' walk across the fields. I believe they serve food and drink."

"Great," said John, happy to be back on more familiar ground. "Is there anything there you'd recommend?"

"I've never been," said Renfield flatly.

"Oh," said John, suddenly thrown again. "Well, we'll let you know what it's like."

"Enjoy your night," replied Renfield coldly. Then, turning to Liz, he said in a smoother tone "If you'd like a nightcap, be sure to come upstairs later. I'm up all night."

The pub served until well after midnight, and the walk back to Renfield Hall seemed much further than the walk there. John fumbled to get the key in the outside lock, already wishing he had not drunk so much ale. With no outside lights, even finding the lock proved a struggle.

"Come on, I'm bursting for the loo," moaned Liz, swaying gently.

"Maybe something to do with drinking two bottles of wine?"

"I needed two to disguise the taste," she replied, wrinkling her nose.

John finally engaged the key and opened the stiff lock. The door creaked open and they both stumbled inside into the dark reception. He felt along the wall for a light switch, and after some prolonged fumbling eventually found it, lighting the hall in a harsh white glare from the fluorescent tubes above.

"I can't wait to get to bed," he yawned, stumbling towards the stairs.

"What about a nightcap with the owner?"

"It's gone one in the morning," laughed John, slowly climbing the steps. "At his age he'll have been in bed since nine!"

"He said he'd be up all night, and I do fancy one last tipple."

"You know what I fancy?" said John lewdly, leering down the stairs and groping Liz's right breast.

"Get off!" she cried. "There's no way we can make love in one of those narrow cots."

"I'm don't fancy making love, it's hot raw sex I'm after!"

"Well, you'd better talk to your right hand nicely then," Liz sneered. "I'm going to the loo, and then I'm going upstairs to see what sort of nightcap Mr. Renfield has on offer."

"A dry sherry if you're lucky," mumbled John glumly. "A cup of hot cocoa and a flash of his string vest if you're not."

"Are you coming?"

"Evidently not tonight," he replied. "You go and get a cocoa, give me a shake when you come back down."

"Give what a shake?" Liz laughed drunkenly, finally reaching the top of the dimly lit stairs.

"Me. And if he has a well-stocked drinks cabinet, come down and get me."

"Maybe," she giggled, heading towards the toilet.

"Enjoy your cocoa," retorted John, stumbling towards his cell.

John woke with a jolt as he hit the floor hard. Stunned and disoriented, he looked around, realising he had fallen out of the narrow single bed of the cell. The early light of dawn filtered weakly through the bars on the window, making the room look even more bleak and Spartan than it seemed the previous evening.

With an effort, he stood, his head still swimming from the alcohol.

"Jesus," he groaned, rubbing his bruised elbow.

Deciding to have a moan about his elbow to Liz, he opened the cell door and limped to the next door room. He found the door unlocked. Pushing it open, he saw the bed un-slept in, the stiff white sheets the same as when they had arrived. He glanced at his watch; five-thirty. Surely Liz must have finished the nightcap with old-man Renfield by now?

With rising concern, he went back into his own room and grabbed his phone, thumbing the button to call Liz. Seconds later, the familiar Apple ringtone sounded from next-door in Liz's room.

"Shit," he gasped, reaching for his crumpled jeans and clumsily dressing.

He went back into the corridor and headed for the stairs, which led up to Renfield's apartments. The steps were narrower, and creaked more than the ones from the ground floor. A dim light at the top of the flight lit his way to a door which halted his progress. He tried the handle only to find it locked.

"Liz!" he yelled, hammered heavily with his fists on the panelled door. "Liz, are you in there?"

A few seconds later and he heard a key in the lock. The door opened and Renfield stood in the gloom, looking as well-dressed as he did the previous evening, but the tweeds replaced by a burgundy satin smoking jacket.

"Yes?" Renfield asked coldly.

"Is Liz in there?" John demanded, looking past the old man.

"She is," Renfield replied suavely.

John looked back down at the old man in surprise, somehow expecting a different answer.

"Do you know what time it is?" John yelled, thinking that he should just barge past.

Renfield calmly withdrew a polished gold pocket watch from inside the satin jacket, flicking open the lid. "It's five-thirty-five."

John stared at the old man, angry and almost lost for words. "What the hell have you two been doing all this time?"

Renfield gave a slight shrug. "Pleasantly passing the time."

"For nearly five hours?"

"Liz is a fascinating person," Renfield replied. "I've really enjoyed her company."

John shook his head, not knowing what to make of it. "Let me see her."

Renfield stepped back out of the doorway into the dim room beyond. "Be my guest. She's in the last room on the right."

Barging past Renfield, John marched down the wide hallway. The layout was similar to the floor below, with cell doors on either side, but the cells seemingly larger. Candles, spaced intermittently in dusty alcoves, gave just enough flickering illumination to light his way. A musty, damp smell permeated the hallway, making John unconsciously wrinkle his nose. The final door on the right gaped open, spilling soft light into the gloomy hallway. Rushing to the door, he looked into the room. Although still a cell, it seemed perhaps three-times larger than the ones on the floor below. Painted in a deep burgundy, with rugs on the floor, a table and chairs, and dour paintings on the wall, it looked slightly more habitable. In the light of the many candles he saw Liz sprawled on the bed, asleep but fully clothed.

"Liz!" he shouted, running to the iron framed bed and shaking her awake.

She looked at him blankly.

"Are you OK?" John cried.

Puzzlement replaced her blank stare, as she propped herself up on the starched white sheets with her elbows.

"She fell asleep after the nightcap," came Renfield's voice from the doorway behind him. "I went downstairs only to find you snoring, so I decided to let her sleep. She looked so peaceful, and so beautiful."

John stood, turning angrily towards the old man. "What was the nightcap — a roofie?"

Renfield looked at him in puzzlement. "I've no idea what spirit a roofie is. I opened a good bottle of vintage tawny port."

"So you just sat and watched her sleep?" John asked accusingly.

"Of course, she is a thing of exquisite beauty," Renfield answered, looking over to Liz.

"You perverted old bastard!" yelled John, turning back to Liz and helping her to her feet.

"Nothing happened, John," said Liz, unsurely. "It's OK."

"Let's get our things and go, we can't stay here with this creep fantasizing over you, or worse!"

Liz held unsteadily onto John's shoulder as he marched out of the room and back to the creaking stairs. He steadied her on the narrow staircase and led her to the two rooms. Within a few minutes they were packed and sitting in the car.

"Do you hurt anywhere?" asked John, trembling with rage.

Liz shook her head. "He acted like a gentleman."

"Maybe while you were awake!" snarled John. "We should call the police."

"No," said Liz. "I don't think he did anything."

John stared hard at her, looking for any sign of wrongdoing. She gave him a brief smile, then her attention shifted to a large brown moth which fluttered against the car windshield, trying to get out. In one quick movement she grabbed the insect and popped it into her month. She chewed, swallowed, and gave John a loving smile.

After thirty years of naval service, **Ross Baxter** now concentrates on writing short stories. He has won a number of awards, and had a story included on the 2017 HWA Bram Stoker reading list. Married to a Norwegian and with two Anglo-Viking kids, he now lives in Derby, England.

www.ingramcontent.com/pod-product-compliance
Lightning Source LLC
Chambersburg PA
CBHW070253310726
48976CB00008B/2645